# WITHDRAWN

## Deer Park Public Library

### Deer Park, Texas

1. Books may be kept two weeks and may be renewed once for the same period, except 7 day books and magazines.

2. A fine is charged for each day a book is not returned according to the above rule. No book will be issued to any person incurring such a fine until it has been paid.

3. All injuries to books beyond reasonable wear and all losses shall be made good to the satisfaction of the Librarian.

4. Each borrower is held responsible for all books charged on his card and for all fines accruing on the same.

JUN 22 '81

# THE MAN WHO MADE EVERYONE LATE

by
YURI SUHL

illustrated by
LAWRENCE DI FIORI

Four Winds Press · New York

*By the same author*
**Simon Boom Gives a Wedding**
**Uncle Misha's Partisans**
**An Album of the Jews in America**

*Library of Congress Cataloging in Publication Data*

*Suhl, Yuri.*
*The man who made everyone late.*

Summary: *Felix Boom has a penchant for making every-one late because of his inability to answer a question in less than five hundred words.*
*I. Di Fiori, Lawrence, illus. II. Title.*
*PZ7.S9445Man    (E)    74–7482*
*ISBN 0–590–7223–4*

*Published by Four Winds Press*
*A Division of Scholastic Magazines, Inc., New York, N.Y.*
*Text copyright © 1974 by Yuri Suhl*
*Illustrations copyright © 1974 by Lawrence Di Fiori*
*Printed in the United States of America*
*Library of Congress Catalog Card Number: 74–7482*

*1  2  3  4  5  78  77  76  75  74*

*To Isabelle*

Once there lived a man named Felix Boom who moved to a new town. He built himself a big house on top of a hill so that when he looked down on the houses below, they seemed even smaller than they were.

One day a townsman asked Felix Boom how many rooms his house had. "I will start with the living room first," said Felix Boom. "It is very, very large. The walls are covered with Indian satin. The floor is covered with Persian rugs . . ."

"I was just asking about the *number* of rooms," the man interrupted him.

"I'll come to that in a minute," said Felix Boom. "Where was I?"

"On Persian rugs," said the man.

"Oh, yes," Felix Boom continued. "And from the ceiling hang three chandeliers, one more sparkling than the other. And there are three sofas covered with the softest leather. Each sofa can seat ten people. In this room there are also twenty chairs . . ."

"All I wanted to know was the *number* of rooms," the man said, impatiently.

"I'll come to that in a minute," said Felix Boom. "Where was I?"

"On twenty chairs," said the man.

"Oh, yes," Felix Boom continued. "And in the center of the room is a large, round table, topped with the best Swedish marble. Now let us move on to the next room."

The townsman glanced at his watch and said, "Excuse me, but I must leave right now or I'll be late for my appointment." And he dashed away.

One day another townsman, carrying a valise in his hand, stopped Felix Boom and said, "Will you please tell me what time it is. I left my watch at home."

"I'll be glad to," said Felix Boom, taking his watch out of his watch pocket. He snapped the cover open and said to the man: "By this watch, which is made of pure gold, and which has twenty-six large wheels and thirty-three small wheels . . ."

"Please, mister, tell me the time," the man pleaded. "I'm in a hurry to catch a train."

"I'll come to that in a minute," said Felix Boom. "Where was I?"

"On thirty-three small wheels," said the man impatiently.

"Oh, yes," Felix Boom continued. "And all studded with diamonds. By this watch which once belonged to the King of Sweden, and later to the King of Italy, and later to a Swiss jeweler from whom I bought it, it is exactly . . ."

"Sorry," said the man. "I must run or I'll miss my train." And he ran off. He ran all the way to the station and when he got there, all out of breath, he saw the train pull out. "If only I hadn't stopped to ask that man what time it was!" he muttered to himself unhappily.

One summer day, as Felix Boom was coming back from the beach, holding a large beach umbrella with red and white stripes over his head, a townsman on his way for a swim stopped him and asked: "How is the water today?"

Felix Boom raised his umbrella up high and said, "On my private beach, which is separated from the rest of the beach by three pointed rocks . . ."

"I was asking about the water," the man reminded him.

"I'm coming to that in a minute," said Felix Boom. "Where was I?"

"On three pointed rocks," said the man impatiently. He was hot, and eager for a swim.

"Oh, yes," Felix Boom continued. "And when I go into the water on my private beach I don't have to step on pebbles and stones but on a soft, sandy bottom . . . "

"But I asked about the water," the man interrupted him.

"I'm coming to that in a minute," said Felix Boom. "Where was I?"

"On a soft, sandy bottom," the man said, looking up at the sky, for at that moment a huge black cloud had covered the sun.

"Oh, yes," Felix Boom continued. "And when I step on that soft, sandy bottom . . . "

"Excuse me," said the man, "but I am terribly hot. I must go in for a swim." And he started to run toward the beach. Just then there was a flash of lightning and a rumble of thunder. It began to rain and all the bathers ran for cover. The man turned around and ran with them, leaving Felix Boom standing there under his large beach umbrella.

Little by little Felix Boom came to be known in town as Felix Boast, the man who gave long answers to short questions, and nobody stopped to talk to him. "What is the matter with the people in this town?" Felix Boom wondered. "They are just like the people in the last town I moved away from. They talk to each other but they don't talk to me."

One winter morning Felix Boom looked out the window of his big house on the hill and saw a whirlwind of snow. "This is a good day to wear my sable fur coat," he said to himself. "The townsmen will be curious to know where it came from and how much it cost." He got dressed in a hurry and went into town.

The wind rattled windows, snatched hats off people's heads and rolled them in the snow. It was very cold. But Felix Boom was warm. and snug in his long sable coat, sable hat, sable ear flaps and sable gloves. With his arms folded over his chest he looked like a huge bear walking on its hind legs.

He strolled to a busy corner where many people were hurrying by. Some, he noticed, were wearing fur coats; here one of rabbit, there one of muskrat, and two or three of raccoon. He alone wore a coat of sable. "Soon," he thought, "someone will stop to admire my coat." But he stood there a full hour and no one stopped.

"This is not a good place," Felix Boom said to himself and walked to the railway station a few blocks away. There he planted himself in front of the entrance and waited. But everybody had heard the story of the man who had missed the train on account of Felix Boom, and so all the passengers hurried past him.

"Out of luck again," Felix Boom thought, and he crossed the street to stop in front of a bakery. He stood there the rest of the morning watching the customers come and go. But nobody stopped to admire his sable coat. Tired and discouraged, Felix Boom decided to go home.

Just then a stranger in town, a young man dressed in a light coat, came out of the bakery and walked up to Felix Boom. "Pardon me, sir," he said, "I'm a furrier's apprentice and I have never seen a coat like yours. Will you kindly tell me what kind of fur this is?"

Felix Boom drew himself up to his full height and said, "Young man, this very expensive coat you are looking at once belonged to a Russian Prince. The Prince had it made for him by the finest furriers in Paris . . . "

"Pardon me for interrupting you, sir," the young man said, politely, "All I want to know is what kind of fur it is."

"I'll come to that in a minute," said Felix Boom. "Where was I?"

"In Paris," said the young man, nervously. It was lunchtime. The workers in his shop had sent him for fresh pastry and were waiting for it.

"Oh, yes," Felix Boom continued. "But the Prince liked to gamble and one day he lost everything he had, at the gambling table, including this coat . . ."

"Kerchoo!" the young man sneezed. He was beginning to shiver in his light coat. "Please, sir," he pleaded, "just tell me about the fur."

"I'll come to that in a minute," said Felix Boom. "Where was I?"

"Kerchoo! Kerchoo!" the young man sneezed again, and he ran off.

"Sable! Sable!" Felix Boom shouted after him. "My coat is made of sable!"

But the young man didn't hear him. Shivering and sneezing, he ran all the way to the shop. "Sorry I'm late," he apologized to the furriers, who were waiting for the pastry. "I saw a man wearing a beautiful fur coat so I stopped to ask him the name of the fur."

"Well, what *is* the name of the fur?" the furriers asked.

"I don't know," said the young man. "He told me about a Russian Prince, and furriers in Paris, and a gambling table, but not the name of the fur. It seemed he would go on forever, so I ran off and left him standing there."

"That was Felix Boom you stopped to talk to," the furriers told the young apprentice. "He's the man who gives long answers to short questions."

"I'll know better next time," said the young man, still wondering what kind of fur it was.

One spring morning Felix Boom rode into town on his new milk-white horse. It was very well trained. One slight touch of the spurs and it went clip-clop-clip on the cobblestone streets. Felix Boom rode up to the square and stopped where all the coachmen stood near their carriages waiting for passengers. "Surely the coachmen will be curious about this horse," he thought, "and they will ask where it came from."

They were curious, but they did not ask. Neither did anybody else. The horse was admired only from a distance until along came a little boy, walking to school with his father. "Daddy, Daddy," cried the boy, "look at that big white horse!"

"Yes," said the father. "He is very handsome."

"May I give him a pat?" said the boy.

"Not now," said the father, who knew that the man on the horse was Felix Boom.

"Why not?" the boy asked.

"Because you'll be late to school," the father replied.

"One little pat won't make me late, Daddy," the boy pleaded.

"All right," said the father, "but don't ask any questions."

"The horse can't talk," said the boy.

"But the man on the horse can," the father said, as he led the boy over to the horse.

The boy had been taught not to touch anything belonging to a stranger without permission. He looked up at Felix Boom and asked: "May I please pat your horse?"

Felix Boom drew himself up on his saddle and said: "This horse, which once belonged to the King of Albania, who gave it as a birthday present to the King of Rumania, who passed it on to his son, the Prince of Transylvania, who later sold it to the King of Spain, who was very vain, who later passed it on to his son, Prince Alfonso the Third, of whom everyone has heard, who made it a gift to the Duchess of Luxembourg, who was pretty and tall but who needed money because that kingdom was very small, so she sold it to the Shah of Iran, who made it a present to Prince Umberto of Milan, who took it on a safari very, very far, all the way to Zanzibar, and who later sold it to a horse dealer in Montana, U.S.A. from whom I bought it one summer day—this horse you may indeed pat."

But the boy stood there and didn't move his hand. He was so confused by all the kings, and princes, and countries which Felix Boom had rattled off that he forgot what he wanted to do. He took his father's hand and said, "Come, Daddy, I'll be late to school."

And he *was* late. Five minutes late!

"Did you oversleep?" the teacher asked the boy.

"No," said the boy. "I stopped to pat a horse, but I didn't."

"Not patting a horse made you late for school?"

"The man on the horse made me late for school," the boy said.

"That must be Felix Boom." the teacher said. "He makes everybody late. This time you are excused."

Soon all the school children heard about the little boy and the horse, and they, too, stopped talking to the man who made everybody late.

One day Felix Boom said to himself: "The people in this town are very unfriendly. Even the children don't talk to me anymore. I am going to move to another town where people will talk to me."

And he did. He sold his house on the hill, gathered all his possessions, including the sable coat and the white horse, and moved to another town.

In the beginning everything went well in the new town. People were friendly to the stranger. They said, "Hello," and "Welcome to our town," and "Isn't it a nice day today." Then one morning a townsman on the way to work stopped to ask Felix Boom what time it was.

Felix Boom took his gold watch out of the watch pocket, snapped the cover open, and said: "By this watch, which is made of pure gold, and which has twenty-six large wheels and thirty-three small wheels . . ."

"I was only asking about the time, sir," the townsman interrupted him.

"I'll come to that in a minute," said Felix Boom. "Where was I?"

"On thirty-three small wheels," said the man impatiently.

"Oh, yes," Felix Boom continued. "All studded with diamonds,

"Excuse me, sir," said the man, "but I must run or I'll be late for work." And he dashed away leaving Felix Boom standing there with his watch in his hand.